I Will Kiss You

(Lots & Lots & Lots!)

Stoo Hample

CANDLEWICK PRESS

CAMBRIDGE, MASSACHUSETTS

I will kiss you everywhere . . .

on your fingers,

on your hair,

on a chair on a stair . . .

on the floor, in the air.

and I'll kiss your teddy bear.

I will kiss you on your hat,

also when you're on a mat,
tumbling like an acrobat.

I will kiss your dog and cat.

Tell me what you think of that.

I'll kiss you when we're at the zoo,
looking at a grumpy gnu.

I will kiss you on your knee
while we're snuggling in a tree
on the sand beside the sea.
No one there but you and me,
just as happy as can be.

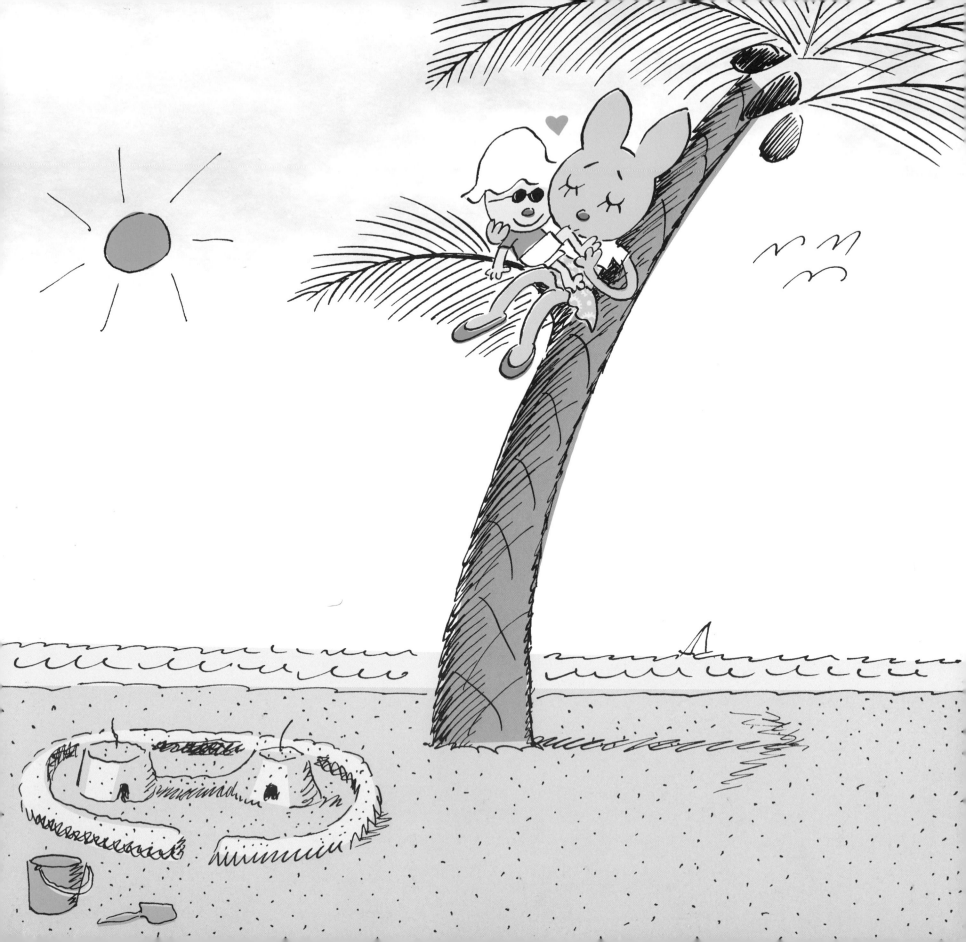

I will kiss you when you fly
your dragon kite so very high –
I mean so very, very high –
that when you see it with your eye,
it looks like it might touch the sky.

I will kiss your tiny thumb
while you eat a cookie crumb

followed by a purple plum.

I'll kiss you when you play your drum
while you're chewing bubblegum.

I will kiss your freezy nose
in the winter when it snows.

I will kiss you on your toes
when you're naked with no clothes
and your tiny tushy shows.

I will kiss you with delight

while we read in bright moonlight

on your bed all fluffy white.

Then, when I tuck you in real tight,

I will kiss you nighty-night.

Any book about kissing has got to be for Martha.

S. H.

P.S. For trying their darndest to make me look good (not easy),
I Will Kiss Joan Powers (fabulous blue-eyed editor)
and Lovely Ann Stott (the wind beneath my wings)
lots & lots & lots.

And thanks to my poetry advisor, Ralph Black.

First edition 2006

Library of Congress Cataloging-in-Publication Data is available.

Library of Congress Catalog Card Number 2005046926

ISBN 0-7636-2787-9

2 4 6 8 10 9 7 5 3 1

Printed in China

This book was typeset in Sitcom.
The illustrations were done in ink and digitally colored.

Candlewick Press
2067 Massachusetts Avenue
Cambridge, Massachusetts 02140

visit us at www.candlewick.com

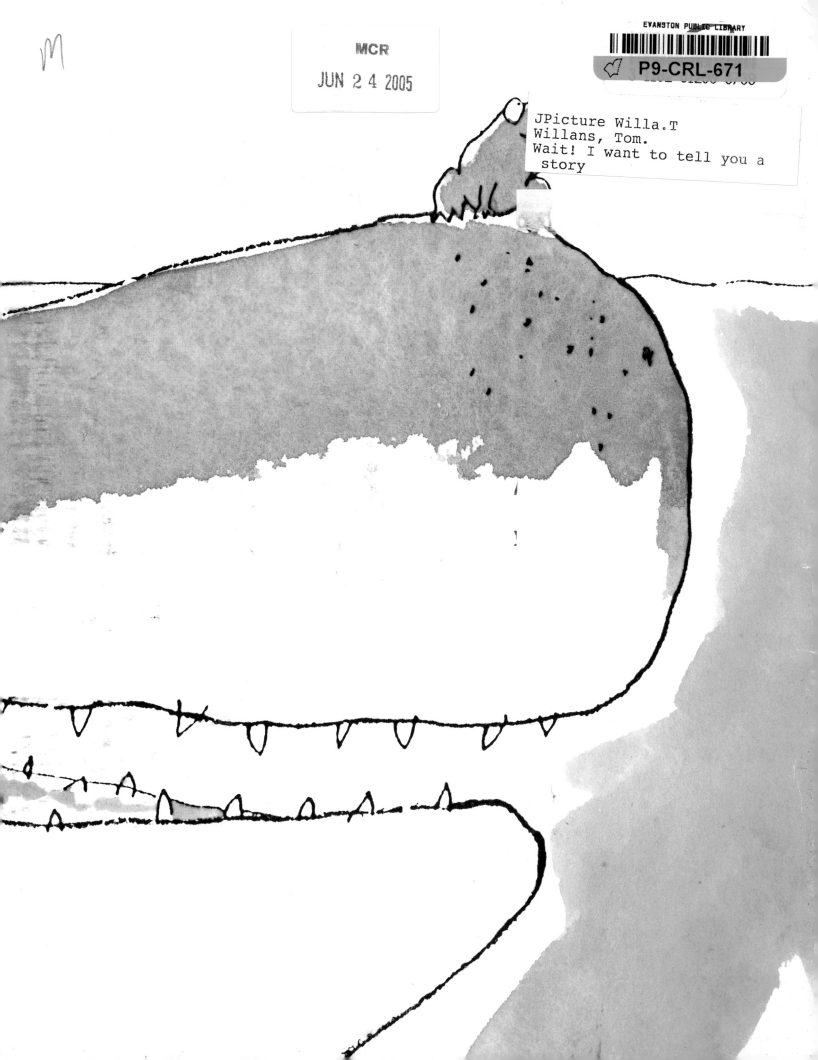

For Mum and Dad

SIMON & SCHUSTER BOOKS FOR YOUNG READERS
An imprint of Simon & Schuster Children's Publishing Division
1230 Avenue of the Americas, New York, New York 10020
Text and illustrations copyright © 2004 by Tom Willans
First published in Great Britain in 2004 by Boxer Books Limited
Produced by Boxer Books Limited, United Kingdom
First U.S. edition, 2005
SIMON & SCHUSTER BOOKS FOR YOUNG READERS is a trademark of Simon & Schuster, Inc.
Book design by Lucy Ruth Cummins
The text for this book is set in Garamond and Priska Serif.
The illustrations for this book are rendered in ink and watercolor.
Manufactured in China
2 4 6 8 10 9 7 5 3 1
CIP data for this book is available from the Library of Congress.
ISBN 0-689-87166-X

WAIT!

I Want to
Tell You a Story

Written and illustrated by

Tom Willans

Simon & Schuster Books for Young Readers
New York   London   Toronto   Sydney

Once there was a muskrat sitting quietly in a tree.

Along came a tiger.

"I'm going to eat you,
little muskrat,"
said the tiger.

"WAIT!"

said the muskrat.
"I want to tell you a story."

"Okay," said the tiger,
"but make it quick!"

"Once upon a time,"
said the muskrat,
"there was a frog sitting on a pond.
A big shark came up through the
water and said, 'I'm going to eat
you, little frog.'"

"WAIT!"

said the frog.
"I want to tell you a story."

"Okay," said the shark,
"but make it quick!"

"Once upon a time," said the frog, "there was a lizard sitting on a rock. A big snake came along and said, 'I'm going to eat you, little lizard.'"

"WAIT!"
said the lizard.
"I want to tell you a story."

"Okay," said the snake,
"but make it quick!"

"Once upon a time," said the lizard,
"there was a fly sitting on a web.
A big spider came along and said,
'I'm going to eat you, little fly.'"

"**WAIT!**"
said the fly.
"I want to tell you a story."

"I don't want to hear it!"
said the spider.
And the spider ate the fly.

"And I," said the tiger,
"am going to eat you, little muskrat!"

"WAIT!"

shouted the muskrat.
"There's more. . . ."

"The lizard ate the spider,

the snake ate the lizard,

the frog ate the snake,

and the shark ate the frog."

"What happened then?"
asked the tiger.

"The crocodile ate the tiger,"
said the muskrat.

"What crocodile?"

asked the tiger.

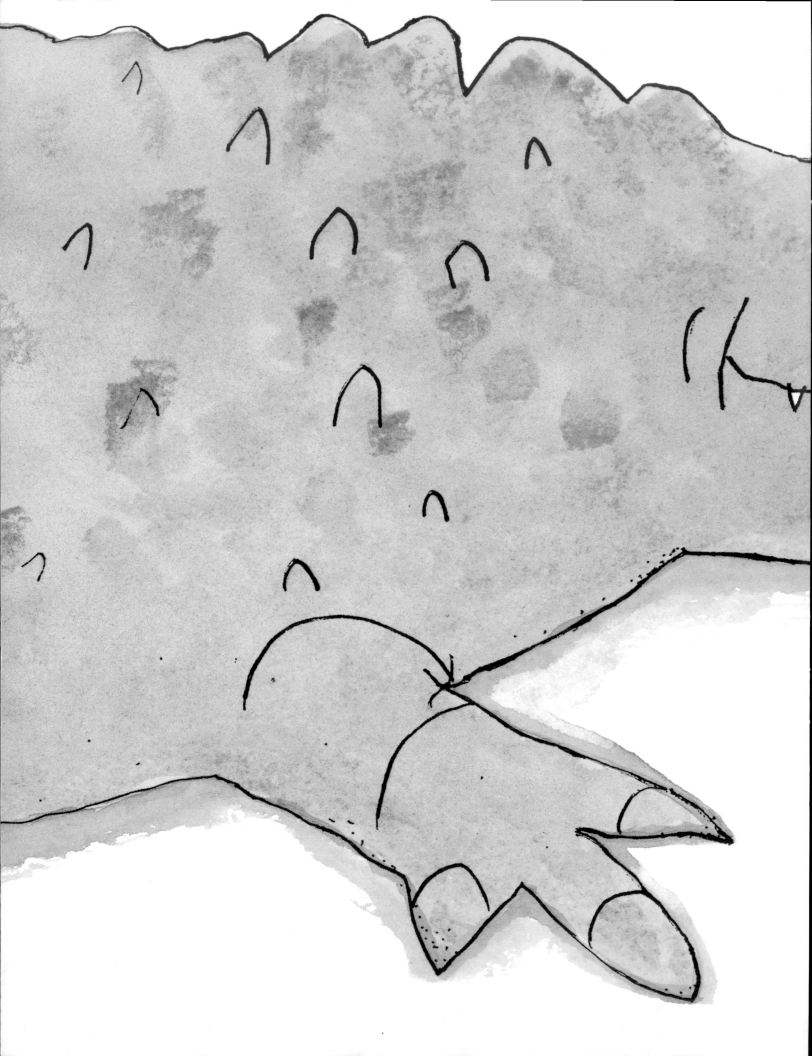

And the muskrat got away.